SCOOBY-DOO!

MONSTERS UNMASKED!

By Nicole Johnson • Illustrated by Red Central Ltd

A Random House PICTUREBACK® Book

Random House New York

Copyright © 2022 Hanna-Barbera.
SCOOBY-DOO and all related characters
and elements © & ™ Hanna-Barbera.
WB SHIELD: © & ™ WBEI. (s22)

Published in the United States by Random House Children's Books, a division of Penguin Random House LLC, 1745 Broadway,
New York, NY 10019, and in Canada by Penguin Random House Canada Limited, Toronto. Pictureback, Random House,
and the Random House colophon are registered trademarks of Penguin Random House LLC.
rhcbooks.com
ISBN 978-0-593-48404-3 (trade) — ISBN 978-0-593-48405-0 (ebook)
MANUFACTURED IN CHINA
10 9 8 7 6 5 4 3 2 1

It was a chilly fall night in Coolsville, and Scooby and Shaggy were walking home from their favorite pizza parlor.

"That pastrami and pepper pizza was amazing, Scoob!" Shaggy said, rubbing his belly. "You know what would go great with that? Ice cream!"

Scooby agreed. *"Ret's ro!"*

The pair turned to head back to the town square—but stopped when they heard a rustling in the bushes.

"Like, that's just a squirrel . . . right?" Shaggy asked.

Scooby sniffed the ground, slowly heading for the bushes. As he got closer . . .

A creepy monster jumped out at them!
"Rawr!" it screamed.
"Ahhh!" screamed Shaggy and Scooby.

Scooby and Shaggy dashed into a nearby abandoned warehouse, looking for somewhere to hide. Rounding a corner, they found a heap of chains on the ground.

"Like, I think we could catch this creeper, Scoob!" Shaggy exclaimed, handing his pal a chain and explaining his plan.

Soon, the monster entered the warehouse and came near their hiding place. Using all their strength, Scooby and Shaggy swung the chains like lassos and flung them toward the monster.

They caught the creature!
"Well, Scoob, would you like to do the honors?"
Shaggy asked his pal.
Scooby walked over and pulled off the monster's
mask, revealing . . .

. . . a different monster!

Shaggy and Scooby sprinted out of the warehouse.
Using another chain, they locked the doors.

"I think we're safe now," Shaggy said.

But as soon as he finished speaking, the pair heard
a spooky laugh behind them.

"MWAH, HA, HA!"

Scooby and Shaggy took off again.
"This way!" Shaggy shouted.
"Ris ray!" Scooby said at the same time.
And in their hurry, they ran in opposite directions!

After a few minutes, Scooby looked around and realized his friend wasn't with him. He began slowly tiptoeing down the street, and when he turned a corner . . .

. . . the vampire was there to greet him! Scooby sprinted back down the block. Seeing an open gate, he rushed through it and into someone's backyard. He thought he'd be safe there.

Meanwhile, Shaggy had escaped the vampire,
but found a mean clown and an angry pirate!

Shaggy led them on a wild chase, eventually losing them in a quiet neighborhood. Feeling tired, he slipped through an opening in a fence to find a place to hide and rest. But he wasn't looking where he was going, and—

BAM!
Scooby and Shaggy crashed right into each other.

"Scoob! I'm so glad I found you, but we'd better get the others," Shaggy said, shaking his head. "This is not a two-person job." Scooby agreed.

But before they could leave and get help, monsters spilled into the backyard from both sides! There was the vampire, the clown, the pirate, and even more monsters they hadn't seen before.

With nowhere to go, Scooby and
Shaggy backed up against the fence. As the
monsters closed in around them, the friends
hugged each other, squeezed their eyes shut
tight, and then . . .

BZZZZT!

Shaggy jumped at the sound of their alarm. He found himself huddled in his bed. It had all been a dream!

"Like, I just had the creepiest nightmare, Scoob," Shaggy said. "But you know what would help me feel better? Pizza and ice cream!"

The pair hopped up and got ready to get some grub.

Later, Shaggy and Scooby met up with their friends Fred, Daphne, and Velma at the pizza parlor. Shaggy told them about his dream.

"It was really freaky, but there's nothing a breakfast pizza can't fix, right?" he said, digging in. He knew it had just been a dream, but he couldn't shake the feeling that the monsters were still out there. . . .